NEEMA'S REASON TO SMILE

BY PATRICIA NEWMAN

ILLUSTRATED BY MEHRDOKHT AMINI

150 East 52nd Street, Suite 32002
New York, NY 10022
www.lightswitchlearning.com

Educators and Librarians, for a variety of teaching resources,
visit www.lightswitchlearning.com.
Library of Congress Cataloging-in-Publication Data is available upon request.
Library of Congress Catalog Card Number pending

ISBN: 978-1-68265-584-9

Neema's Reason to Smile by Patricia Newman
Illustrated by Mehrdokht Amini
Edited by Adam Reingold
Art Direction and Book Design by Paula Jo Smith
The text of this book is set in Apex Sans.

Printed in China

For Annette and Kelley
and for the inspiring students at
Jambo Jipya School in Mtwapa, Kenya

Mama and I climb the hill to our favorite rock overlooking the savanna. We dream of the future while elephants take mud baths in the fading light.

I want to go to school, but without money,
I can only dream.

"You could be a nurse," Mama says.

"Or a scientist," I say.

We empty our pockets. One coin ... then others ... until they jingle with the promise of dreams come true.

Mama counts out coins for our beans and rice.

One lonely coin remains. I put it in the Dream Basket that Mama and I made for my school money.

The next morning, Mama balances a heavy fruit basket on my head. "Off you go, little one."

Mile after mile, my bare feet trace the dusty path that unwinds like a cheetah's tail all the way to town.

"Oranges. Mangos. Bananas," I call over the rumble of matatus carrying passengers.

“Two oranges, here.” The corn man drops coins and an ear of corn in my hand. “Still not in school? Do you want to be like me and roast corn your whole life?”

“Mama and I are saving for the government school.”

“That school is free,” he says.

“But uniforms, paper, and pencils are not,” I say.

I nibble one corn kernel at a time in the shade of the spice shop. A girl in a red skirt and white shirt skips by.

A thought buzzes like a mosquito. The girl wears red and white, but government school students wear blue and white. The buzzing grows louder. Is there another school in town?

The girl springs like a gazelle past the chapati woman selling breakfast. One hop … another … down the crowded street.

I follow her, basket balanced. One careful hop … another … down the street, but the chapati woman calls to me for mangos. By the time I pocket my coins, the girl is gone.

Another day, I start for town on the dusty path. Again, I see the girl wearing red and white. She walks the log bridge, her arms spread like egret wings. One step … another … across the creek and into town.

I inch onto the log, my basket heavy on my head. One wobbly step … another … across the creek and…

I stop to give the toothless old beggar his daily orange even though he cannot pay.

“The heart of a lion beats inside you, Neema,” he says.

My heart roars for the girl and her school, but she is gone.

“Oranges. Mangos. Bananas.”

The water man struggles to push his heavy cart up the street. "One banana, little one," he says in his sing-songy voice.

"Still not in school? Do you want to be like me and peddle drinking water your whole life?"

"Mama and I are saving for the government school," I say.

The water man points to a group of tourists. "They look hungry for fruit," he says.

I run home up the dusty path, my basket empty.

I sweep the yard and gather firewood. Mama sews dresses for the shop in town. Her needle flits like a dragonfly.

Before sunset, we climb the hill to our rock. She empties her pocket, and I empty mine. One coin … then others.

Mama counts enough for our flour and corn. I put three others in our Dream Basket.

That night, as Mama sews by the light of the fire, her last good needle breaks. “I am sorry, Neema, but I must buy new ones.”

Together, we open the Dream Basket and take out what Mama needs. Will I ever have enough coins to make my dream come true?

REPUBLIC OF

Days later, when the chapati woman hands me her coins, I see the girl in red and white again.

I follow her as she weaves through the crowd on the noisy street.

She dances through an open red door and into school.

One twirl … another … across the courtyard and past boys and girls reading books like zebras nibbling sweet grass.

I pause, my basket still full of fruit. My heart thumps one time … another … and then roars with hope. I clutch my basket and follow.

Suddenly, the girl stops. Will she tell me to leave?

Instead, she takes my hand. “I am Asha. Welcome to my school.”

She shows me a library with shelves of books.

“Teacher Madam, a visitor,” Asha calls to a woman who stands tall like a proud acacia tree. Her smile gives me courage.

“Fruit, Bibi?” I offer her a ripe mango.

Teacher Madam gives me a coin. “Do you go to school, little one?”

“Mama and I are saving for the government school,” I say.

“I see,” Teacher Madam says. “Come tomorrow with your mama. I have an idea for you.”

Please put the books away properly!
Wildlife
Math
Literature
Geography
Science

Sitting on our rock on the hill, I tell Mama about Asha and Teacher Madam and the library.

I see disappointment in her eyes when I give her my few coins.

We empty the Dream Basket.

"Are there enough?" I ask.

Mama shrugs. "I do not think so, little one."

"I would not need to ride the matatu," I say. "That will save money."

Mama's smile is full of hope. "Someday, you could work in an office."

"Or be an inventor," I say.

That night, we toss and turn on our mats.

At daybreak, we walk hand-in-hand down the dusty path to town. Can Mama hear my lion heart roar for school?

Through the red door, Teacher Madam weaves a bright future of lessons and books and two meals a day.

But Mama shakes her head. “How much for uniforms, pencils, and paper?”

“Pay what you can. We provide the rest,” Teacher Madam says.

"Neema found us because you sparked her desire to learn," Teacher Madam says. "Let us give her the skills to make her dreams come true."

Mama turns to me. "How will we live without your fruit money, little one?"

"I can sell fruit on my way to school," I say.

My hand tightens on hers. "I could be a teacher."

"Or a doctor, " she says.

Teacher Madam hands me a white shirt and a red skirt. Mama empties the Dream Basket into Teacher Madam's hands.

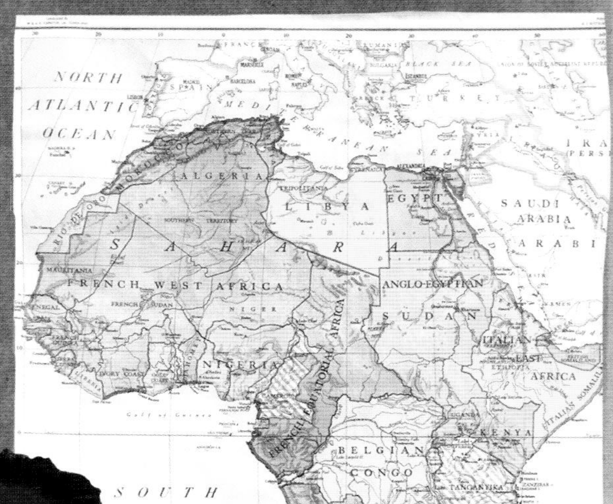

I perch beside Asha on a
crowded classroom bench,
a new member of the flock.

Teacher Madam shows me how to write one letter of the alphabet … another … from A all the way to Z like a lizard's dainty footprints.

In the library, I flip pages … one book … another … hugging each one to my chest.

After school, Mama and I run up our hill. I give her the empty Dream Basket. “For your sewing machine dream, now.”

“With a sewing machine, I can work faster and take in more work,” Mama says.

“You could make so many dresses,” I say.

“Or run my own business,” she says.

One day after the rainy season, I put on my white shirt and red skirt. I start for school on the dusty path that unwinds like a cheetah's tail. A girl with a basket of yams on her head follows.

I walk the log bridge, my arms spread like egret wings. One step … another … across the creek and into town.

The girl inches onto the log, her basket heavy on her head. One wobbly step … another … across the creek and into town.

Outside the red door, I stop and smile at her.
"I am Neema. Welcome to my school."

OUR DREAMS

Do you think about the future like Neema does? Do you know what you want to be when you grow up? Jambo Jipya students share dreams from their Dream Baskets.

"To travel the world and go to many of the places I see in the movies …"
—Shadrack, age 11

"To become a nurse, work in a hospital, and help people …"
—Grace, age 17

"To study engineering and maybe even become a pilot …"
—Manasee, age 12

"To build things with my hands and have my own business one day ..."
—*Mark, age 13*

"To do well in school and go to university ..."
—*Mary, age 15*

"To open my own salon and make women feel good about themselves ..."
—*Ashora, age 19*

"To visit the United States, especially New York ..."
—*Emmanuel, age 10*

Discussion Questions

1. Why doesn't Neema go to school? Why does she want to go to school?
2. Why is the Dream Basket an important part of the story?
3. The author writes that Neema's bare feet "trace the dusty path that unwinds like a cheetah's tail." What does that mean?
4. Neema talks about several things she could do when she grows up. What do you want to do when you grow up? What skills will you need to achieve your goals?
5. Neema sells fruit to help Mama. Do you have any responsibilities to help your family?
6. Neema gives a toothless man an orange every day even though he can't pay for it. Why do you think she does this?
7. Why do you think Neema's mother is disappointed as described on page 22?
8. What does the author mean on page 25 when she writes, "Through the red door, Teacher Madam weaves a bright future of lessons and books and two meals a day"?
9. How does the classroom shown on page 27 look similar to your classroom? How is it different?
10. At the end of the book, Neema welcomes a new girl to her school. How do you welcome a new student to your school?

Activities

1. Write a story about a person who dreams of a better future. Describe how the person's dreams did or did not come true.
2. The toothless old beggar tells Neema that "the heart of a lion beats inside you." Draw a picture describing what his words might mean.
3. Neema's mother works hard to save money so that Neema can go to school. Make a thank-you card for one of your parents or any other person. The card should offer examples of what he or she does for you. Include examples of actions that let you know that he or she cares about you.
4. What is a goal or dream that you have? Write a step-by-step plan describing how you will achieve your goal.
5. Write a poem describing what your neighborhood looks like in comparison to Neema's community. Include at least five words from the glossary on page 36 in your poem.

Group Activity

Create a Dream Basket

Students should work with a partner to create their own Dream Baskets.

STEP 1 Cut a piece of 8 1/2" x 11" construction paper in half along the width. Each piece should measure 4 1/4" x 11".

STEP 2 Draw a design for the sides of the basket on the two pieces of construction paper.

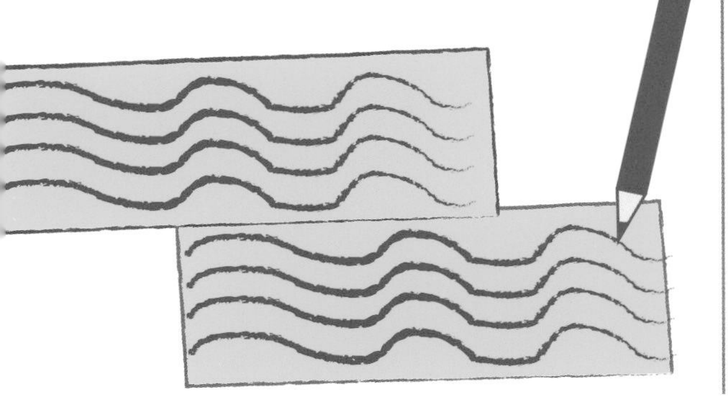

STEP 3 To make the sides of the basket, tape the ends of the papers together along the width, first measuring that the two pages overlap each other along the edge for 1 1/2".

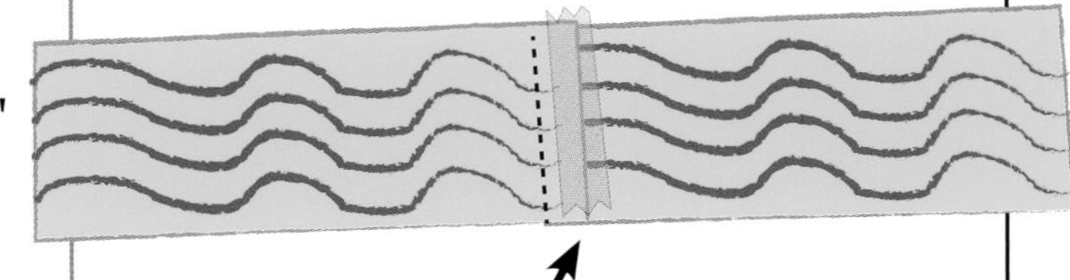

When taping ends together, be sure they overlap by 1 1/2".

STEP 4 To make the bottom of the basket, use a pencil to trace the bottom of the basket on another piece of construction paper. Then make a second circle about 3/4" around the outside of the traced line.

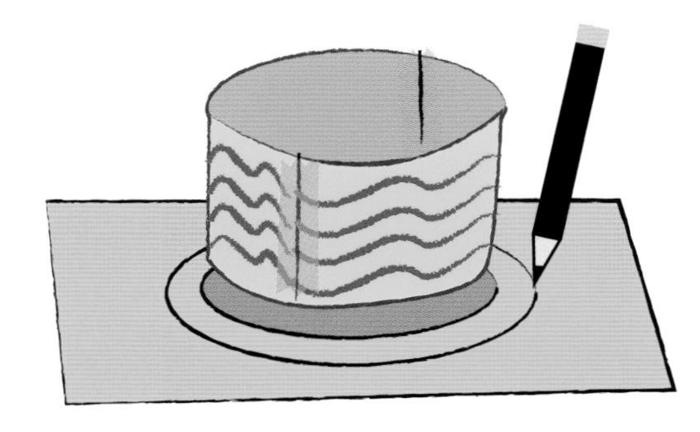

STEP 5 Cut along the outer circle, then cut slits from the outside circle to the inside circle. Fold the slits inward.

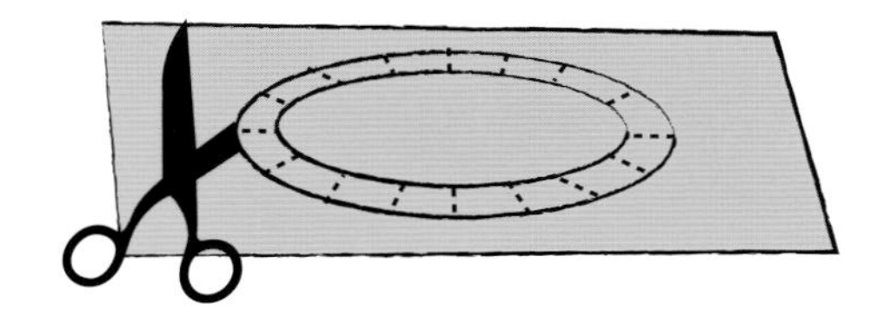

STEP 6 With a partner, push the bottom into the basket, then tape the slits to the inside of the basket.

STEP 7 To make the basket handle, cut a 1" strip of construction paper lengthwise. Tape it to the sides of the basket.

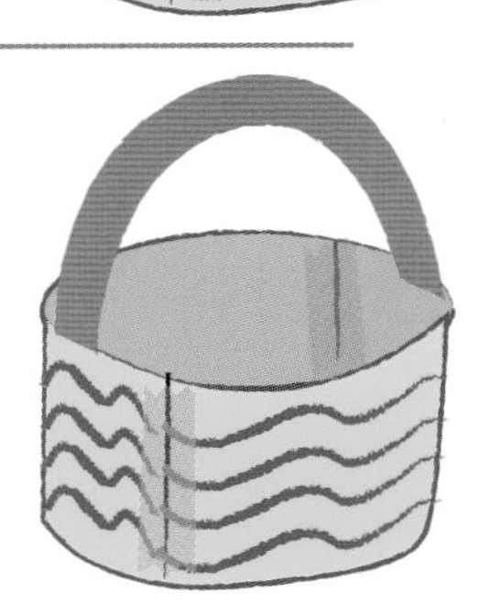

STEP 8 Write out your own dream or goal on a small piece of paper to put in the basket.

STEP 9 Present your unique Dream Basket to the class, making sure to read aloud your own dream.

GLOSSARY

Acacia *(noun)* a kind of tree that has yellow or white flowers *(p. 20)*

Bibi *(noun)* word used to politely address a woman, such as *Miss* *(p. 20)*

Chapati *(noun)* pancake type of flat bread from India *(p. 9)*

Courage *(noun)* bravery and strength *(p. 20)*

Courtyard *(noun)* an open area surrounded by a building *(p. 19)*

Dainty *(adjective)* small and beautiful *(p. 28)*

Disappointment *(noun)* a feeling of failure *(p. 22)*

Dragonfly *(noun)* a kind of insect with big, clear wings *(p. 15)*

Egret *(noun)* a white bird that eats insects stirred up by the feet of large animals *(p. 10)*

Fading *(adjective)* losing brightness *(p. 3)*

Flits *(verb)* to move quickly and lightly *(p. 15)*

Flock *(noun)* a group of birds or a crowd of people *(p. 27)*

Flour *(noun)* ground grain used to make breads and cakes *(p. 15)*

Inventor *(noun)* a person who makes something no one ever made before *(p. 22)*

Jingle *(verb)* to make a soft tinkling sound *(p. 4)*

Kernel *(noun)* the soft part of an ear of corn that you eat *(p. 8)*

Mangos *(noun)* a yellow and red tropical fruit *(p. 9)*

Matatu *(noun)* a small bus *(p. 6)*

Needle *(noun)* a thin piece of metal with a sharp point at one end used for sewing *(p. 15)*

Nibble *(verb)* to eat in small bites *(p. 8)*

Peddle *(verb)* to try to sell something *(p. 13)*

Perch *(verb)* to sit on something *(p. 27)*

Savanna *(noun)* a big grassy area with few trees *(p. 3)*

Scientist *(noun)* a person skilled in science *(p. 4)*

Skills *(noun)* the ability to do something well with practice and experience *(p. 26)*

Tourists *(noun)* travelers *(p. 13)*

Trace *(verb)* to follow a pattern or line *(p. 6)*

Twirl *(noun)* the act of spinning around *(p. 19)*

Uniforms *(noun)* the same clothing worn by people in one group *(p. 7)*

Weave *(verb)* to twist and turn from side to side *(p. 18)*

Wobbly *(adjective)* moving shakily from side to side *(p. 10)*

From the Author

Story ideas come from a lot of different places. The idea for *Neema's Reason to Smile* grew out of a phone call with Donna Rosenblum, a librarian from New York. One of my author friends suggested to Donna that I would be a good fit for a project about the power of education. Donna picked up the phone and called me.

Donna told me about Christine Mwende and the town of Mtwapa, Kenya, where many kids are unable to go to school. Sometimes, they are too poor to buy the uniforms and supplies. Other times, their parents don't understand the importance of formal schooling. Christine opened Jambo Jipya School because she believes everyone has the right to learn. She works with the chiefs of many Kenyan tribes to convince families that education is the key to a well-paying job and a better life.

Donna introduced me to Keela Grimmette who used to work at Jambo Jipya School when she was in college. Keela loved the school and the children so much she started an organization to help raise money for food, books, and more modern classrooms. Keela called her organization Reason2Smile (www.reason2smile.org), and Donna now runs it.

To write *Neema's Reason to Smile*, I asked Donna and Keela and Christine hundreds of questions. I'd been to Kenya before, but I needed to understand Jambo Jipya School. These dedicated women spent many hours on the phone with me. I watched videos of the kids and studied their photos. I saw how they handled life with grace and perseverance, and I wanted my seven-year-old main character to be like them. In fact, I chose the name Neema (NAY-ma) because it means "grace" in Swahili.

Neema's Reason to Smile is a work of fiction, but it is based on the real-life students at Jambo Jipya School who understand the power of education. I hope their story gives you a reason to smile.

Acknowledgments

Thank you to Donna Rosenblum, supervisor of School Library Services for Nassau BOCES and Executive Director of Reason2Smile, and Keela Grimmette, founder of Reason2Smile, for their generosity and for their unwavering support of the shared dream in our Dream Basket.

Additional thanks go to Christine Mwende, the real-life Teacher Madam of Jambo Jipya School, and her inspiring students who give all of us a reason to smile.

May you always have many reasons to smile and share them with the world!
Keela Grimmette